Hamish
and the Missing Teddy

Moira Munro

Piccadilly Press · London

Hamish was off to the Great Teddy Bear Picnic with his small friend Finn.
He waved goodbye to his special little girl.
"It's her birthday today," he told Finn. "As her special bear, I want to take a terrific present back to her."

Finn leapt up. "What does she like best?"
"Ribbons for her hair," said Hamish. "But you can't find ribbons at a picnic! Help me think of something else."

But Finn just wanted to play.
He jumped on to Hamish.
"Catch me!" he squeaked.

Hamish wanted some peace and quiet to think
of the perfect present, but he loved little Finn.
So they played aeroplanes . . .

and racing cars . . .

brrrr!

and bouncy bears . . .

bing!

boing!

and Hamish had no time at all to do his thinking.

All the teddy bears helped to take the food out of the picnic hamper and sat down to enjoy the Great Teddy Bear Picnic.

Hamish kept trying
to think of a present,
but with Finn bouncing
around, it was very difficult.

Just as Hamish was about to tuck into a big slice
of raspberry cake, he finally had an idea.
"Cake! That's what I'll give my little girl," he thought,
and he placed it carefully next to him. But then . . .

with a leap,

zoom!

...a spin

whee!

...a somersault...

whish!

and an almighty **backflip,**

Finn landed . . .

...right onto Hamish's cake!

wham!

"Oh no! You squashed it!"

shouted Hamish. "I was going to give that to my special little girl!"

"I'm sorry," whispered Finn.
"Don't worry," said Hamish kindly, "it was only an accident."

"But I squashed the present!"
And the little bear's eyes filled with tears.

"We'll think of something else," replied Hamish with a smile. "Just you wait."

Two bears asked Hamish to join them in a race.
Hamish didn't notice that Finn was still upset, and off he
went, without his friend.

Finn was left all alone.

"Hamish is so cross.
He doesn't love
me any more,"
he thought.

"I'm just a silly,

small

bear,

who bounces too much . . . and squashes presents."

The other teddies were so busy playing that nobody
noticed Finn was missing until it was time to go home.

Everyone was so worried. All the bears joined together in a search for Finn.

"Finn!"

"Finn!"

"Where are you?"

Hamish was especially anxious.
"Finn is so little," he thought. "I hope
he's not in trouble."

Hamish ran this way and that,
calling for his friend,
louder and louder, and
just as he was running
out of breath . . .

"BOO!"

Finn leapt out of the picnic hamper.

Hamish jumped.
"Finn! I'm so glad you're all right! Don't you *ever* disappear like that again! We've been so worried."

"I thought you didn't love me any more," said Finn.

Hamish hugged his friend fondly.

"You can love someone and still get annoyed when they squidge cakes!"

Finn skipped happily.
"Look what I've found in the picnic hamper! For
your little girl!"
Hamish gasped. "Two gorgeous ribbons! Why that's
the perfect present! You're some bear, Finn."

"I promise I'll never, ever bounce again!" said Finn.
"*Ever!*"
"Oh, please don't promise *that*," said Hamish. "Your
bounce is what I like best! Your bounce is what makes
you YOU!"